25 Letters Later

Ally Molison

Copyright © 2022 by Ally Molison.

All rights reserved. No part of this book may be reproduced in any form or by any electronic or mechanical means, including information storage and retrieval systems, without permission in writing from the publisher, except by reviewers, who may quote brief passages in a review.

This publication contains the opinions and ideas of its author. It is intended to provide helpful and informative material on the subjects addressed in the publication. The author and publisher specifically disclaim all responsibility for any liability, loss, or risk, personal or otherwise, which is incurred as a consequence, directly or indirectly, of the use and application of any of the contents of this book.

WRITERS REPUBLIC L.L.C.
515 Summit Ave. Unit R1
Union City, NJ 07087, USA

Website: *www.writersrepublic.com*
Hotline: *1-877-656-6838*
Email: *info@writersrepublic.com*

Ordering Information:
Quantity sales. Special discounts are available on quantity purchases by corporations, associations, and others. For details, contact the publisher at the address above.

Library of Congress Control Number:	2022944411
ISBN-13: 979-8-88536-856-8	[Paperback Edition]
979-8-88536-873-5	[Hardback Edition]
979-8-88536-857-5	[Digital Edition]

Rev. date: 08/04/2022

Chapter

1

A spark, A Flash, Then light. As my father lights a candle on a cold night in December. My father Lit the candle daily because my mother died on December 13th. He does this because he's always wanted the best for me. Now every night, he lights the candle she made for him. He sometimes has a hard time some nights letting the candle, so I help him. I know we're not the Wealthiest, but he tries his best on the farm, and for me, he wants me to help sometimes, and when he does, I help. Father is a lovely man, but he didn't use to be that way. My mother met my dad. She said he was beating up some guy that pushed you out of the way. She's with some friends; they were just out for a smoke with a dog. See, my father was popular and perfect back then; he was the town's bully. He hit everyone that got in his way or his friends. You can probably tell he has gotten softer through the years. That all started the day, my mother met my dad. It was their first day at church and their first day of class. My mother and father were in church together; the teacher made them do a class project. Let's just say they both hated each other.

You see, my father is mean to everyone, including girls. He had two girlfriends then and made sure no one talked to them. He likes owning things, and of course, he owns them. My parents spent nights and days working with each other because of his church project; they fought but also got along well. You see, my father started to fall in love with my mom during the weeks and years of seeing each other. So he finally decided to change for her. He had fallen so deeply in love with her and wanted her to see him that it took him over ten years to change and ask her out. I mean must have been true love because she said yes. After church one day, he finally asked her to marry him. A few years went by, and they had me. There was happiness but some sadness. When I was born, I had a lump on my head that went to my brain. The doctor said that I only had a day to live. My parents begged to bring me home the doctors finally agreed. My father always told me my mother would sing me songs when I couldn't sleep. I only knew my mother for a few years. After a few days and years, I overcame whatever disease I had. When I was cured, I was only five; my parents were happy but were keeping something for me. I could tell based on the look on my mother's face. Now I know why my mother cried on my dad's arm the day I turned 6. She had a lung disease from smoking all back then. My father did everything in his power to keep her alive, but she died on December 13th, three days before her birthday. My father always used to blame me for my mother's death, I knew he was angry and didn't mean what he -said, but it still hurt his words. Ashamed, it almost reminded me of his younger self. My friends would wonder why I had scars on my back. I always made an excuse for my father because I knew he never meant to hit me. He was just drunk and hurt. I learned how to cook and clean for my mother, to whom I promised to take care of them. She used to always laugh at that. My father used to love my laugh because it sounded like hers but doesn't now. Some days I go to her favorite spot to see the stars, I always ask my father to come, but he just looks and takes a sip of his drink. When he did that, I was most comfortable with my best friend, Colette. She was probably my best friend in the world, and she used to make me the best cake in the world. She knows that my dad hits me; she can tell by me walking into church some days. She was learning to be a housewife because she used to care for me so well. I always loved the way she cared for me. I spent most days and nights at Colette House away from my father. My father never liked her or her parents, so I usually told him I was just going camping to look at the stars so he didn't hit me. My father is not so fond of rich people because of the way they used to treat him. I know my dad makes shit Money, but everything he does is for me. He spent almost all his money on a carriage so that I could go anywhere instead of walking miles. I tried to give him gifts when money presents itself, but we're from women are not allowed to work. The only place you can perform is a laundry place in town, But we make a penny a week. Colette is a fortunate girl in

3

my eyes, She tries not to show how much money she has, but sometimes she slips up. I never get mad when she does. I just smile and tell her how beautiful the dress she's buying looks on her. my father used to say I got my mother's heart. I used to always laugh when he said that. Back then, he was laughing with me; now, not so much. Nowadays, even going to church is a challenge because all I do is laugh and talk to Colette. We got in trouble a lot which usually means we got hit in the hand by a ruler. Colette and I have the same thing about the number of ruler scars on her hands. She used to call them scar tattoos, even though I never really knew what she meant when she would call them that, but I never questioned it. Colette would always make me take home cake and water when I had to return home. She would also give me some money so my dad would be happy. I never liked when she did that, but she is too powerful to say no to. My ride back home was a 5-minute carriage ride back. I always send a letter to my dad when I return from a trip. I do it because he waits for me at the steps to greet me and hug me. Then we cook some pig that I get on my way back. He treats me like a queen when I return from trips. He used to do this with my mom. My father doesn't get out anymore; when he does, he's gone for months or years. He works with the army, so when they need him, he goes; whenever he leaves, I invite Colette over for some tea and cards. When she makes the trip, I can never sleep; I'm just awake anxiously waiting for her arrival.She helps me with the housework my dad

25 Letters Later

left for me to do. She always makes the most wonderful meals for me as well; she takes such good care of me but never allows me to take care of her. She always says I cared enough for my mother to last a lifetime. I always used to smile and laugh at that. She always told me how much I looked like my mother and how she loved my laugh. I wish I could say Colette was more than a friend now, but in my mind, she was just a best friend.

Chapter 2

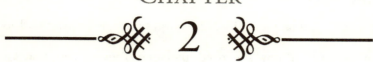

Tik-Tok, swoosh, bang. I woke up from the wind hitting my window. I always wanted to fix that window, but my father won't let me. I know it was dark out early Friday morning, about 3. I knew my father would get home in 2 hours. I tried to sleep, but the wind was too loud. So instead, I sat up and wrote about the Stars I saw that night and what they meant. See, my mother used to name the stars that differed from each other in the sky. That's where we used to spend most of our time together. I spent most of my time writing till I heard the pitter-patter of my carriage horse's feet. When I heard that, I ran downstairs, got some cake and tea, and laid them on our table. I waited by the steps as he walked to me. He told me he had a surprise but was hungry, so I brought him inside. I ate my breakfast fast so we could tell what the surprise was, but instead of telling me, he put me on a hunt as he sat there and drank tea. It took a while, but I got to the last clue when I opened it. It was a trip to see my grandparents down West, which was a 13-hour ride. I was so surprised my dad wanted to see his parents, but I ran to my room and wrote a letter to Colette about where I was going. I always kept her updated so she won't worried about me. My dad's relationship with his parents is very complicated. His parents were wealthy and wanted him to take over the farm in business, but he was only allowed that if he got married to someone his father approved of. When my father introduced my mother to them, his mom and dad said no the minute they saw her. My father tried to tell him that she would help the farm business, but his parents said no, so he had a choice to follow his heart or respect his family that night. Well, in my opinion, he made the right choice that night. My father and I only saw our grandparents once every 15 years, so my dad gave us the chance to see them. The day we were leaving for a long carriage ride, Colette came by a few hours before we would go. She brought over some cake and tea for my father. Even though my father never really liked her, he still gave his best to her some days. Colette wanted to help me pack, but my dad had always been against two girls in the same room, even if it was for doing some cleaning. So I made her go back home and told her I would write her every day until I returned. I never knew what she did with all of my letters; maybe I thought she threw them in the fire, but I guess I was wrong. My father made me some meatloaf before we left for a long journey. I always loved his cooking, even if all he could make was meatloaf, unfortunately. My mother was always the better cook and parent to me; she would always welcome Colette to come over and let me bring her to my room. I think she knew something about Colette just by how she was always accepting when she would come over. I never thought anything of it. I liked my mother even more when she would cook for Colette and me. She always made the best ham with mashed potatoes and her signature gravy. Anyone that had my mother's food would fall in love with it. Clear one night was so good and bad you could not forget it. It was Colette 10th birthday, and her family was having a big party but they invited my family but at that time; my mom was very sick and couldn't make Colettes favorite meal. So I offered to help make it. I always loved cooking for Colette, and then I finally could make my mom's special gravy. When I was done, my father made me walk there by myself. The journey was long and hot but I got the right as the party started. Colette's mother helps me with the food, and Colette draged me to dance with her. We danced for hours but never got tired. I enjoyed the time until the guy on the horse who delivered letters had a letter for me. It was from my father. With a shocked look, I opened it fast and read, so fast that words were a scramble. The only words clear in my head were; Your Mother is dead." When the words hit my heart, I fell to the ground holding the letter to my heart. As no one knew what had happened. Colette ran to me and read the letter. She sent me home, and her carriage held me tight as I cried into her arms. As I got home and ran to my mother's dead body and sang one of the songs, she used to sing to me. My father joined me as we pushed her body into the river under the high stars. That day, my father paid attention to me in a loving way. I never told anyone how I found out my mother died. I kept it a secret until now. My father was the smartest in his family, so his parents wanted to give him the farm. I talked about how he would do so well, but only if he married well. My father always hated when they said that because he wanted to marry someone that he loved, not what his father loved. After going on and singing sounds in my head, we finally made it to my grandparents. I always loved visiting them because they always bought me new clothes and fun toys. As I ran to knock on the door, my father unloaded our stuff. My grandma came to the door, and I gave her the biggest hug and her two dogs. I always had a great relationship with them and never was more me than with them. I found my grandpa in In the yarn smoking when he saw me he put it out and hugged me, he said he did have a surprise for me, As he said that I jumped for joy and was hoping it was a new dress because I needed one. I ran to help my father bring our stuff in. Then we sat down as my Grandpa handed me a big box with a cute bow; I asked my father to help me because he never opened their presents for himself. When I opened it I saw a bright sparkly red dress. I took it out and asked my father if I could put it on. Yeah, he said it was all right. My father was never into it expensive dresses or clothing but liked when I was happy. I knew that with this dress, my father and his father would get into some kind of argument. After putting on the dress, I came down for some tea with my grandma. At that point, my father and Grandpa went to his office for private time. My grandma loves spending time with me. She always asks me about Colette's friendships. My grandma liked Colette just like my Mother did. I think it was how good she cared for me and looked out for me. Over the hours, we talked about my and Colette's life. Over the talking, we heard yelling and bangs from the office my father was in. I didn't question anything until my father came out drunk, looking like a train had hit him. I know you should never say anything when he's like this, but he's been bleeding, so I asked what happened. A mistake I learned right there and then at that moment. Not only did my father yell at me, but he also raised his hand and made a fist. My grandpa ran over to him as my grandma ran to me on the ground, showing me to the bathroom as my grandpa and father yelled and hit each other. I asked my grandma what I did wrong, and she said I did nothing wrong. She washed my face for me and told me to sit down. My grandma knew I wouldn't forget what had happened that night, so she thought it would be better if she told me why we had been there three years earlier. I was initially confused, but it made a little more sense when she explained why we were there. when I had that lump in my brain, it was always hard for me to understand what people were saying. The only words I understood for my grandma were, "He's not on the will, and he'll have to marry someone of his father's choice to be allowed back into this house." I always asked why does it have to be Grandpa's choice who my father had to marry.

25 Letters Later

I was scared of my father and grandpa, so I never said what was on my mind when I was around them. after my grandma explained, I went to my room and wrote a letter to Colette so she'd know what happened. I knew that when she read it, she wanted to make sure it was alright, but I told her it was dangerous for her to come in my father's state. I didn't speak to my father anymore that night or the next morning, and he said I wrote more about the moon and stars. My grandma was like my mother; she would come with me and help locate the different stars. I wanted to talk to my father, but I hesitated to remove with my grandma. who the day I'm going to talk to my father and Grandpa wants. My grandma made sure I was happy, though.My grandma made me wash up so I could make some dinner. She knew how much I like to cook, so she let me choose what to make. Of course, I went with my mother's dish. Even if my grandparents didn't like my mother, she loved her cooking. My grandma would always mention how I was just like my mother. I hope I get the table set and my dad and Grandpa. my father said he was sorry, but something changed in me this time. I just hugged him and made him sit down. I think he knew so what happened with him showing his true colors. As we ate, I didn't look or talk to him. It was quiet, just like it was at home. After I was done, I told my grandparent's goodnight and went to lie in my bed. Before I could, my grandpa stopped me and handed me a letter. From my mother, the day she passed, I opened it but couldn't read it, so my grandpa helped me. It was saying my father had gotten cold again by getting drunk every night and hitting her. the only words I understood were 'he never cared for me.' My grandpa read out loud. I just wanted to cry, but no tears were com. Instead, I was outraged. I remember I told him him thank you, I told him i was going to write to Colette, He looked at me and smiled. And he held my hand. I smiled and said I was sorry. That night I didn't know why but I still wrote to Colette; I told her everything my grandpa did and got me; I also told you the letter about my mom and dad. I never mentioned what my father did to me later in the day, but I think I kept it a secret so she wouldn't worry even if I needed her the most right now. I went to bed even though my mind was wandering the next morning. I woke up to my father packing my stuff and drinking. Instead of asking, I just helped him out. I thought about my grandparents and told him to thank them for the dress. I made sure to tell my grandma my mother's recipe. Has I got on the carriage and thought about what Colette was doing as the horse pulled the carriage away from my grandparents.

Chapter

3

As we made our journey home, I watched the snow come on the carriage's windows—the first snow in 3 months. I love playing in the snow and also protecting it. Colette and I used to throw snow at each other through the years. However, my father never really liked the snow and would not let me go out and play in it. Throughout the journey home, my father said nothing to me. If he talked to me, it was only to ask for a smoke or another drink. I tried my hardest to speak to him but got short answers. Finally, I dared myself to ask what my grandpa had said to him that night I got hit, but I stuttered and kept it in. I reminded my father of our first snowstorm with my mother. I was helping my mother milk the cows When all of a sudden, my father ran in and got me to come outside with him. Well, of course, in such a hurry, I went to get my mother. Has snow fell, we all watched; we all watched the snow make for farm wet and shiny. That day was the only day I saw my father so happy that it was cold outside. When I returned that memory to him, I saw a little smile from my father. That's the only good reaction I got from him the entire trip. A few more hours went by, and the snow fell even more. It fell quiet again in the carriage. I was too bored to sit anymore, so I made my father stop the carriage; not only could I spread my legs but enjoy the weather. He refused at first but finally let me go. I wanted to make the carriage ride back home fun, but it was a little tricky; you see, I was so mad at him for hitting me, and he was still mad at his father. I always wondered what happened in that office that day, I know my father can get angry, but the way he was that night was very different. That night he was already drunk and mad about how long the ride was to get to his parent's house. I didn't bring it up; I kept it in, but I remember it as a night I will not forget. When I stepped in, the fluffy cold snow reminded me of the day Colette came running to me. She visited me on November 20th in the afternoon, the expected time. Colette came, Only this time she came running to my door, Started knocking like a mad woman. At first thought, something terrible had happened because she struck so violently. But she was excited to hang out with me in the snow. Put on my coat and told my parents goodbye, we went to Colette's house to hang out, and I didn't either. I do have to say it was enjoyable, considering how cold we were. Her parents were very nice to me. They even played some music so we could dance together. I like dancing. She was good at it, but I didn't like it as much as she did. That day she was very clingy to me. She was all over me, but I didn't care as much because we were having fun. My father interrupted my memory by saying we had to get back on the journey. My father never liked exploring or enjoying the cold weather or even weather in general. All he wanted was to drink and work on his farm. I'm more like my mother than my father, and I can live like that. Besides, Colette likes everything I like, but as my father grew eagerly mad, I got back in the carriage so we could start on the trail again. Like before, my father said nothing to me, so I decided to break the quiet and ask him what happened that night with his father. He stared at me for a while before answering. He told me his grandpa was dying and wanted my father to have the house and money. My father would have to get remarried to someone his parents picked out, and we also had to leave our farm and all of our animals behind. My grandpa wanted my dad to get rid of everything he worked so hard for just for my father, to earn money and the business. My father declined as well as saying that he would never remarry someone. I finally understood why he was so mad that day. My father also mentioned that he was sorry for hitting me. At first, I just Shrugged It off; but it was my father's face. I forgave him. my father started to ask questions; now it wasn't so quiet. He wondered about Colette's family and her, which surprised me a lot, but I told him they were both good, happy, and healthy. We were almost home, and my dad stopped to get us some food. He also mentioned that we would have welcomed home parties. I always loved when he would spoil me even if we were not doing our best. After the long 13-hour ride, we finally made it home, and my dad cooked us a meal. as tired as I was, I made it up the stairs, into my bed, and finally fell asleep.

Chapter

4

The following day my father woke me up. I laid in bed thinking it wouldn't just be a little thing; I was feeling a lot, and it was taking my entire brain. Still, I don't know what I was thinking to this day. Either way, I got dressed and went to help on the farm. My father was more chilling and talkative than he was yesterday. He did order me around even though I knew what I was doing. We're working a young man came over with five letters to my father, as a young boy handed a note over my father asked if you would like to get to know us better. I was shocked and surprised that he would ask someone he didn't know. One thing is he was a boy coming into our house. My father knew him or something. My father barely allowed Colette in our home. The Young man smiled at me, but I just turned away. My father handed me the letters as he went inside to make some team. All the letters were for me. They were all from Colette. The young boy came over and sat beside me as I started reading. Uncomfortably I Got up and asked what he wanted. He stared at me for a few seconds, then mentioned he was waiting to know why I had so many letters. With a disgusting look, I told him my best friend. Afterward, I went to my room to be alone and read my notes privately. When I opened 1, the words used melted my heart. Each word touched my heart somehow. Cut words were very inspiring to me. When I couldn't see her, I always returned to all the letters she sent me. I kept every single one of the letters she wrote To Me. I read all of her letters and then went to see her. I mean, it's better than being with a young boy I didn't even know in my father. I grabbed a carriage end left who's time in a hurry, so I got there in no time, and no time was wasted. I ran up to the door and knocked then someone came, have your annoying time she finally came to my to the door. as the door opened and I saw Colette I jumped into her arms and gave her a big hug. after a while she asked how my trip was I gave her a standard answer of fine. Colette knew me too well, and she knew I was lying, but you never questioned it and left my answer where it was. She decided it would be best if we made some cake and tea. Colette not only liked cooking but also when we failed at our baking, which reminded me of when Colette first gave me the title of best friend. Around July, Colette sent me a letter to come to her farm. When I got there, she offered to cook with me even though I told her multiple times I could never cook. That time she looked at me, laughed, pulled me in close, and whispered that she didn't know how to cook. I laughed at her, and she left as well. We walked into the kitchen and just eyeballed the ingredients to make the cake. As we tried putting it in the oven to cook the cake, it exploded all over us. When that happened, we laughed so hard that we fell to the floor. We lay on the foundation for a while, and at that moment, Colette rolled on top of me. Initially, I was nervous, but as she got closer, I felt less anxious and more of a relief and comfort. Before she could do anything, her parents walked in, and she got off of me, and I quickly mattered too. We both laughed as we cleaned up the big mess. The day she wanted me to spend the night, I first said no because we had changed my mind. Colette helped me Focus whenever I would space out thinking of old memories. Whenever I spaced out, She always asked what I thought even though, most of the time, I didn't tell her the correct answer. This time I told her the memory of us. she laughed and put her head on my shoulder. I did the same before her mom walked in, wondering what we were doing. Colette told her we were making cake and tea. Her mom just looked at us both and smiled before going outside. Colette tapped on my shoulder, and as I turned around, I felt the soft touch of lips hit mine. When I opened my eyes again, I dropped everything and said goodbye as I jumped into my carriage, still in shock about what had just happened. I thought on my way home that if my father found out what Colette had just done, I would be dead and her. I stopped when I walked into my house and ran to my room. My father stopped me and asked many questions about where I was. I gave him the simplest of answers. Until he looked at my lips and asked where I got lip gloss. I passed me told him no one, but he pulled me by the color of my dress and said

"You Do Not Lie To Me." I quickly tried to pull away, but his grip got stronger. Finally, after enough of me trying to pull away, he gave up and showed me into my room. He quickly slammed the door as he walked in. I kept telling him that no one kissed me, and the lip gloss was from no one, and it was only mine. But he did not believe me. He grabbed me again; this time, it was harder and more demanding as he asked again and again. This time I said nothing. At that point, he lost his mind, and his hand went up and back across my face. I wanted to fall, but his grip was so firm that it kept me up. I tried to pull away, but his grip got stronger and stronger, as well as his hitting. There he hit me five more times before pushing my body to the floor and leaving. It took me a minute to get back on my feet and start walking again. When I finally did, I went to the mirror to see how bad my face looked. When I looked, they were five lines on my face from where his nail scratched me. I also looked at my shoulder, which had five holes from his grip. I thought it was worth keeping Colette safe and not telling him she kissed me. I kept telling myself to make myself feel better despite hurting. I went to the side of my bed and wrote a letter to Colette telling him what my father did; I didn't forget to mention her kiss. I told her I was sorry for running away and that I was scared. As I sealed it, I gave it a little kiss, gave it to the mail-boy, and told him to deliver it quickly.

As I walked back, I went into the kitchen, and my dad was waiting. He asked one last time what was on my lips. Even though I saw him take off his belt to get ready to swing, I stood there and told him again that no one had touched me. He stared at me and smiled and took a drink, and said.

"I told you not to lie to me." Those were the last words I heard. After that, everything went black. All I remember is hearing my screams as the metal part hit me in the rips and legs. I tried to get up and run, and my body was so we could hurt. I only made it to the door. as I closed my eyes again, all I could think about with my father, someone I loved continuing to hit me and hit me even though I was bleeding. After 15 minutes of this abuse, he stopped and picked me up. Hehe hugged me and then pushed me into my room. My body was too weak to stand. I just fell by the bedside. I just lay there in pain, having no one. As I closed my eye,s I heard my father yelling at someone in the rows downstairs. I'm trying to get to the dorm the films, but this time, someone caught me in their arms, resume leave being able to see out of one eye, I got a glimpse of the face. But I wasn't sure until I heard their voice. They said to me, be calm, and he won't hurt you when I'm here. Very quietly, I asked if it was Colette. Her voice said yes. I wrapped my arms around her and gave her such a big hug that I almost fell on her. Add me back, but in a more typing, trying to figure some my hair trying to call me down, it took a while, but when I finally calm down, she wants me to the bathroom to wash up. I asked her softly why she came here

Ally Molison

when I told her it was dangerous. She took a deep breath and told me she could not let her best friend suffer for what she did. I kept telling her that I never said anything about what she did, she looked at me and smiled and told me to be quiet she cleaned me up. as I got cleaned up I went through a letter she gave me, she had in fact about me 100 letters, and somehow I kept all of them. I realized that one of the letters I had never opened when I saw it Colette stopped me, telling me that I could only open it on the 25th of December. Ask her what was so important on December 25th, and she just smiled and told me you just wait and see. I told her before she left that she must come to pick me up and bring me to her home. All Colette did was hold me as I fell asleep in your arms.

Chapter 5

As the morning sun peeked through my room into my eyes, I heard the soft rain hit the roof of the house. As I got up, I could barely stand and put on my dress. As I put on my dress, I heard the mud spider coming with her horses. I got ready as fast as I could and went outside. I was walking out. I never once said anything to my father, and Colette helped me on the horse as I made my way. After that, we're on our way to Colette's house. Colette said nothing to me as we rode, just an occasional smile. The rain kept pouring down as we rode, but the sun was still shining. You could smell a long way or flowers in the very relaxing shower. Colette stoped at some well. I looked at her confused as you took a penny and threw it in. She looked at it for a while until she heard the coin hit the water. She returned and explained that she had made a wish put only she in the well knows. I laughed a little, but I told her I understood, As more time passed through our journey to Colette's house. Only this time, I stopped for some tea and cake, But I managed. Reset it for a while as more rain started to come down. We didn't care. We liked the shower as well. as we finished, we got back to Colette's horse, this time no stopping after while we finally made it. I Got down and took off my shoes to enter the house, as Colette walked the horses back. as I walk through the door, her mother had opened it. Colette told me her mother already knew why I was there; she just hugged me and set me down in the kitchen. Colette's mother told us to go to the bedroom before her father came home, so we did as we were told, but as I sat, She handed me a box. It was very weird-shaped and heavy as well. As I opened the box, all the letters I had written to her fell out. I was shocked that I had written that many, as well as her keeping them all. As I put the letters back and handed the box back to her, I told her I wanted to stay until December. She grabbed my hand and told me I could only last for a month. I smiled at her Sushi knew I understood. Before anything, Colette made sure I was happy in the room. I told her I was and that I felt safe with her family. She smiled and hugged me right then her mom called us to lunch. We hurried down and into the kitchen. As I walked closer, I smelled something very familiar. But when I saw it on the table and melted my heart, what's mother made my mother's famous dish that I love so much. As I sat down, her mother kept coming out with more food. I sat there in shock as she made all my mother's meals. Finally, her mother said that we could eat when everything was set. I grabbed the first plate and put every dish I could find on it. As I put food in my mouth, all I could taste was the love in perfection that her mother put into the meal. It wasn't long after Colette, and I had finished the meals. After dinner, we have to wash all the plates and wash up ourselves. Colette,asked if we wanted to play cards. I told her I would do anything with her. After a while, she gave in and played. After awhile Colette's dad walked in. When he did, we stopped to help him bring in the milk in the wheat he got from the farm. Working with them felt like a family, and working with my father. She took care of me and acted like I was their kid. Either break sweats fathered wonder what I was doing there, I stood there trying to tell him what happened, but nothing was coming out. Colette noticed and stepped in, telling him everything In detail. After she was done speaking, he came over to me and grabbed the milk bucket out of my hand. I just had it on the ground. He hugged me, told me I was brave, and kept my mouth shut. No one knew what happened with Colette and me, but Colette and I shared never to tell. After helping Colette's father, we went back inside to wash up. Whatever was done, I went inside the barn and climbed on the roof. I lay there for a while and waited for the stars to come out. I was there till it was pitch black. Colette came up to the roof to see where I was and what I was doing. I told her i was just waiting for the Stars so I could write about it. Colette smiled and took my hand and kissed them. then she told me that she was happy that I was her best friend. I laughed and asked her why she was happy I felt like I had made her life a mess. but I always had a way to make me feel better. She knew that I didn't understand things because of my disease, but talk to me in ways I understood. After talking to her, we got down and headed to her room. When we stepped into her room, she told me to put on my gown and get some sleep. I did what she wanted me to do when I lay in bed and closed my eyes. I was asleep. Colette woke me up the next morning, making sure I slept well. After my mother passed, I told her this was the best sleep I had gotten. I got dressed and ate some food before heading out, helping cut and her mother. we're from the girls had to get the eggs from the checks and clean the house, and on laundry days, we had to do the laundry. As Colette's mother clean the house. Me and Colette went to get the eggs. We use to race to see who could get more eggs the fastest. I always used to win, but color found a way to cheat, so now she wins most of them. I have to wash the eggs and cook them while Colette set the table. After cooking, I put out the food right then Colette's father walked in with the milk. As we ate it all up, we helped to clean it up. Colette took me aside and said they were leaving for the north and won't be back next year. I took her hands and asked her why she was going so far away from me. She told me that she was moving where women are more accepted. I told her I would write every day until I could visit her. She smiled at me and said

"When The 25th comes around, open that letter." I nodded and smiled at her. After a long day, I washed up and started to pack up. I, unfortunately, have to go back home tomorrow. Colette gave me one last

25 Letters Later

time before we went to bed. I whispered to her that my dad knew it was you stop. Instead of saying anything, she looked at me and nodded, almost as if she understood, as I went to my bed and lay there for a long time to close my eyes. The following day I set off home, but I got one last hug from Colette. I said my goodbyes and headed home.

Chapter 6

As the wind howled, I saw my house and father standing by the stairs. When I looked at him, he had a big smile, and as he helped me off my horse, I hugged him. he told me he cooked his favorite meal while waiting. When he told me that, I rushed inside, and there it was on the table, his favorite meatloaf. I ate the whole plate until it was licked clean, and there was no crumb you could see. He grabbed my plate and smiled, and I gave him another hug. I went up to my room to unpack. My father gave me a letter the young boy had left me. The minute my father handed it to me, I threw it on the bed because I didn't want to read it. My father told me I had to or would be hit and punished. I accepted but asked if I could unpack first before opening it. He nodded his head, then left back downstairs. After unpacking, I looked at the letter for a while, wondering if I should open it. I finally gave in and opened the damn letter. Most of the words I blocked out, but there was one sentence that caught my eye very clearly. The young boy mentioned that my father was waiting for me to get married. After I saw that I threw the letter to the ground and hurried downstairs to talk with my father. Of course, as I walked into the kitchen, he was just sitting there drinking as usual. I asked him very nicely what the letter was about. He looked at me and told me when I turned 18, which had already happened on the days I went with Colette, I had to find a boy to marry me, even though I made it clear that I wanted nothing to do with marrying a boy and to only live on the farm. I had to marry this boy just because my father liked him. I didn't argue with him because I did not want to be hit and punished today. Instead, I walked back upstairs and wrote a letter to Colette to see what I should do. Even though I knew she would not have an answer for me, I still did it. After I was done writing, a little jealousy came over me. I was jealous that Colette was not only moving to somewhere that respected women more but also that her parents were making her not get married. I went back down to tell my father that if he made me marry this boy, he would never hear from me again. He nodded with a little smile and told me the boy was coming to pick me up tomorrow. I was so shocked that you didn't care how I felt anymore, unlike you used to. Before I left to work on the farm, I told him that he was never my favorite father and that Mom was way better. All we did was smile at that comment. I felt the most hurt is such a kind man could be so cold again and meaner after something he couldn't control. Also, to think that I covered up for him and supported him when I was younger. I guess an abuser is always one and never a good person. I left my father to tell me and order me around the rest of the day. I let him even though he had no intention to order me that day. I felt like a slave, but I think I just waited for the day to be over because the next day, I left my father behind to go with a little male boy I had only met once. Even though I was mad that I had to marry a boy, is better than staying here and being abused. After a long and grueling day, my father finally allowed me to wash up and change. I made one of his and my favorite meals for one last night together. Even though I didn't say anything to him, he told me thank you for the last time. As I made my way upstairs, he stopped me. He didn't say anything, just stood in my way for a few minutes before saying.

He said you were always strong. I picked up my clothes and writing utensil before heading to bed. My dad woke me up the following day and said he was sorry. I nodded and told him I knew. Then we set off.

Chapter 7

During our trip, I asked the young boy what his name was to get to know him a little better. He told me it was Daghan Which means a good-hearted person. At first, I didn't know what he meant by that, but I smiled a little as you told me his family was from Ireland and moved for better farm life. I asked where we were exactly going. He mentioned we were going to his parent's farm so I could meet them. Then we would make our way to his farm. I was excited to meet new people and learn more about Daghan, a young male boy. He stopped at every Landmark, telling me its history of it. He made the carriage ride fun and enjoyable instead of dull and miserable. I still didn't want a new friend or fiance, though. I asked him what he thought about marrying someone he barely knew. He told me he was used to it. I guess his parents made him get married several times but never really liked the girl till he met me. I laughed when he said that because I was insulting and not willing to talk when I first met him. I guess he likes girls that were hard to get the attention of. He told me to look in the side of a carriage where he left his mail. I asked him why. He told me there's a letter for my best friend. Of course, he did not know her name because when I first met him, I only gave in the answer of best friend. When I got the letter I told him thank you, I have to say he was very kind and respectful to women. Daghan told me when we were done meeting everyone. He would take me to Colette's new house. At first, I wondered how in the world he knew where Colette lived. But I smiled and hugged him when he said that. I opened the letter and read it very slowly. She told me how nice and big her new house was. Colette also mentioned that she was sorry about what my dad had done in making me marry someone I had just met. A little smile came through, and Daghan asked if it was good news. I told him it was and also said what she told me. He told me I had a good friend and I should never lose her. I smiled even more, but he told me we were there right then. As I looked at it, I only saw such a house in beautiful grass. Not only was the place so vast and beautiful the grass was so green that the air you smelled was so lovely. This is the house I have always dreamed of, just based on beauty and character. As we got closer to his parents, they started to walk out of the house. As we stopped, Daghan helped me out of the carriage and walked me up to his parents. I felt like a queen when he did that, but I showed my respect as we got closer. His parents both bowed to me and shook my hand. This was the first time someone had treated me with this much respect. They invited me in and brought me to their living room. As I bowed in appreciation, their helper took my jacket and clothing to my room. As I sat down with Daghan, I asked whose house this was. I got a very thoughtful response from his mother, saying it was his. I looked at him and smiled. This place was twice the size of my farm and house. His mother asked me a lot of questions about where I was from and All the answers were given as his father walked in. I stood up and bowed to him as he told me to sit. Daghan parents were very powerful-looking people. I didn't know what they did, but I never thought to mention it. More questions were asked, and answers were given. As it was time for his parents to go, we walked them out and bowed as they left. When Daghan couldn't see his parents, he asked me if I would marry him. Quickly I answered and told him no and that I needed to get to know him better. Smiled and said he was joking and agreed with me. I asked him if we could go and see Colette, he nodded with a smile. On our way there I asked a lot about how he got that house and what his parents did. he didn't give me a lot of answers on it only that his father knew the king of England. I was surprised when he told me that but I respected his wishesto stop talking about it, Daghan How a my father used to treat name. I told him that my father used to be a kind man but when my mother died he became cold again and abused me. He laughed as he said

"I'm glad I got u then" When he said that comment not only did I laughed but I also agreed. Not long after he said we were there, I told him that we were not even that far away from are house. All except the door and knocked after the first not open the door and came running into my arms, she hugged me tight as I did the same. I introduced her to DaghanAnd I had to marry him. she had a smile but did not like the idea of me getting married. I invited Daghan in but he told me he would wait outside. My hand and took me to her living room were they were playing music. If I would dance with her and despite being tired I would always dance with her. She smiled as she took me by the waist and move my hands to hers comment pause the music got louder it filled my heart knowing I was by someone that loved me Never told me she loved me her actions spoke for herself. When the music stopped hold me close closer and whisper to me not to forget her. I reassured her that I would never forget her no matter how far away we are from each other. I'm at work I had to go but as she insisted she gave me a peace offering oh, a peace offering of cake and tea comment on my way out I told her I would visit every other day. as I set off with Daghan I look back to see if Colette was still standing there and with my luck she was with a big smile on her face near her door, I told Daghan That I would be with him if only he respected and appreciated me. He took a deep breath and agreed. I hugged him and we smiled and laughed all the way back home. I knew that I didn't love him or like him but it was better than being back to my father. I think we both knew that both of us didn't like each other but we kept her parents happy and that's what mattered. When we made it home Daghan gave me a tour of the house in the farm, everything was so taken care of and beautiful. I did ask if he wanted me to help out on the farm or only in the house, he looked and told me I could do whatever as long as things are kept clean and precise. We talked on and on about our parents and how they treated us, we seem to have a lot in common especially getting forced to marry someone you just met. I told him through the hours of work that he must keep me away from my father but close to Colette. He understand me but still ask that I clean and do laundry before going to see Colette. I smiled and told him I would and respect him. He did forget to ask if I knew how to cook so I showed him I could. Down a pretty plant down of my mother's ham and mashed potatoes. He told me my father said I'd liked to make this meal, I gave him a smile and made up. After dinner he walked me to my room and waited till I was unpacked and comfortable before he left to his room. I sat on my new bed wearing and thinking about the day I have to get married. It took a while for me to sleep and when I did it felt so good and I was so comfortable. The next morning the sun peeked through my windows and woke me up. I made sure to clean the house and do my part before asking Daghan To go see Colette. He smiled and nodded for my approval awesome telling me I did not have to ask for permission anymore. I smiled and started to walk to Colette's house. As I made my way I heard bugs buzzing and bird singing it was such a peaceful walk through the woods. Through halfway though I saw a clip walking towards me come she didn't see me at first so I yelled to her. When I did she looked up with a smile and ran to me. Fashion girl clothes when I held up my hands, which she grabbed then let go to hug me. We laughed as we fell on the soft grass oh, I asked what she was doing walking to my house she told me she was coming to see me even though I told her I would always going to see her. She laughed and asked which house we should go to since we were by both. I insisted that she come to mine for some lunch and Music oh, I also told her to get to know the Daghan a little better. And took my hand as we walked back, all I remember that walk is how happy she was in her bright smile. I always was alive and smiling with the clap when she left everything went away. As we walked in my front door Daghan stop us What I was doing back so early, I explained what happened and he laughed. I invited him in. And to come with me and Colette for some dinner. he agreed but after he was done with the cows. Colette offer to help me with the tea but I made sure that she just sat there and waited. When Daghan Came into the kitchen he gave me a kiss on the cheek for the first time oh, but I did not see the discomforts and jealousy run on Colette's face when he did so. once he did it a couple more times I did see Colettes face and jealousy so I made him stop. Colette helps get the table and helped me into a chair, as we ate I introduced Colette a little more to Daghan And likewise about Daghan to Colette. As we where getting done i told Daghan that he should treat himself in town. My cheek and she said goodbye to me and Colette in left with the carriage. Clint help me clean up but wanted me to be with her even more. I could tell by her movements in face that she wanted to be with me, as any good friend I granted her that wish and turn the music on for her. By then she did the rest with with my hands and her hips. We dance till night, but then left when Daghan walked in. On her way out that she would come back in the next week time. I said goodbye as she left. Even though this time when she left I felt so empty but i put a smile on for Daghan. As he walked to me he grabbed me by the waist and hands as we danced again. My heart was still hurt so I told him to stop as I left to make us dinner. he paused before asking me how my day was with Colette, I gave him a brief answer of good, After that he left to go feed the pigs and animals as I made him dinner. I had to remember that I had to get married tomorrow even if I refused. I was onlyn 18 yeras old I didn't know how to be a housewife or helper, More about it than I did. I need to tell Colette that she would get married and I'd be living with my parents. I guess the tables turned. But either way I still had a wedding tomorrow, as I finished I sat out Daghan Food and went up to bed dreading tomorrow.

Chapter 8

The sun peeks through the kitchen windows, making the flowers open up. As Daghan was preparing the animals for killing, I was stuck writing letters to people I wanted most to come to our wedding. I made sure to invite Colette but not my father. I could not bear having him thereafter everything. I ensured everyone I invited, My future husband, liked it as well. We sat and talked about how we felt about it. We both laughed as we went through the list. To me, it felt like I was marrying my friend. I smiled at him and returned to work I had to do as he did the same. We didn't talk much during the day, though I never got a letter from Colette nor saw her walking from the hill down to our house. As I washed all the plates and silverware I thought about Colette and what she was doing. I was very tempted to see her but knew I had work to do and promised Daghan I would do that right before traveling. I can't tell if I felt something for Colette. I always remember the letter she told me not to open but knew it was so tempting to read what it said. But throughout the day, my mind became less focused on Daghan and the wedding. So

I Turn to my writing about the different stories in the stars that greatly relate to people. To me, each star has someone different in life with their personality. I spent most of my day writing until Daghan returned from the farm. He did leave me alone to my thoughts when you first walked in. I had to stop thinking before my mind went somewhere else, so I decided to go cook instead. I do have to say I respected my future husband's family. They overwhelmed me because I knew nothing about them when I first met them. He asked if I would make my mother's favorite dish for the wedding. I told him yes because I need people to taste what my mother used to cook even though she's not alive anymore. I never told him what happened to my mother; I only made sure that I gave him a few answers about how she died. The next morning our wedding was starting as I got my wedding dress on and ready for myself. Daghan brought people to their seats and sat them down. when I was done, I heard a knock at my door. Before I let them in, I made sure it wasn't him. the voice I heard was very soft and quiet. I told them they could come in, still not knowing who it was. As the door opened I saw Colette standing right there. She had such a big smile on her face, and without any hesitation, I ran to her and gave her the biggest hug. I whispered to her and said

" I didn't think you would come," She told me that she would always be with me on special occasions and for the rest of my life. I told her I wanted one last dance with her before I got married, she smiled as she grabbed and put my hands on her waist. she got close to me this time I didn't flinch, she got very close to me, but I never stopped her, and she pulled me even closer to her she whispered to me, though I couldn't hear it because of the music downstairs, instead, Colette told me it was in the letter name 25. After that she went back downstairs, as Daghan mother came to walk me down the aisle, she took my hand. I smiled and told her that her son is a very liked man who greatly respected you. She smiled and told me that I was a lucky girl. As we made it downstairs, she handed me off to Daghan so we could walk the rest of the way together. I smiled at him as the pope made us wife and husband. He gave me a kiss on the cheek and then walked me to the kitchen to eat. Everyone throughout the night drank and laughed and danced. I remember seeing Colette dancing and having a good time as she did. It put a smile on my face to see her that happy. I think she knew I was happy that I was no longer with my abused father, which made her even happier. When she came to eat and talk to me, she mentioned me making a family and being a mom. I had to reassure her that I and Daghan barely touched each other and left each other alone most days. She asked me to dance, to which I said yes. The rest of the night, Colette danced no matter how tired or even looked at us. she danced to the last person who left your house before she went home. I offered to walk her back, but Daghan told me to stay and see some rest. I didn't like what he said, but out of respect, I went to my room and lay in bed. The next morning I woke up to the smell of fresh muffins getting pulled out of the oven. As I made my way downstairs, my husband stopped Me, took my hand and walked me to sit in the kitchen. I was so confused, but he did not hint at what was happening. He told me to sit and eat and get ready to travel somewhere magical. I gave him a look but ate up and got ready to go. he helped me in the carriage and then told me to go to Colette's house. I smiled and told him goodbye. During the short ride there, I couldn't wait for whatever they had planned. When I got up the hill, I saw Colette standing there with a big smile. as I stopped, she jumped in and hugged me. I asked her what she had planned so the only answer she gave me was that we were going east to see the beautiful stars together. Once you told me that I was so happy and my smile could not be hidden. Colette already knew how much I like the stars, and seeing them was one of my dreams. I had to ask her why she was doing this, but every time it was going back to the 25th letter she wrote me. I was curious about what she had written in it but kept my promise to only open it on the 25th. On our way there, she gave me little hints about what we were doing there. She did tell me that we were going to stay there till December 25th. I asked him if my husband knew, with slight hesitation, she shook her head no. I smiled and agreed and said great. I asked her a lot of questions about life throughout the trip. I mean, this trip was a whole month just to get East. On our way there, we never got bored or tired. We were happy that we were together and alone. Throughout the trip, we saw cute and scary animals and learned something new every day. Colette didn't let me do much. Instead, she took care of me and stayed awake while I slept. She pulled away even if I tried to take it from her so she could sleep. I appreciate everything she was doing for me. Sometimes it was very painful and hard for me because I still have scars on my face and eyes. When I would tell her I was in pain, Colette would put some water with a hit of mint in it. In my personal opinion, I didn't think it worked, but I loved her determination to help. a few hours passed, and we stopped in town to get food and water. so I learned not to trust Colette to go alone in town because she had a cute puppy with her when she returned. Colette said it was for me. At first, I thought she was joking, but she continued our journey. I spent the most time playing with the puppy till we got there. After a long trip, we were finally at the picnic with the best view of the Stars. Colette helped me out and got me down on the blanket. I have no idea what she planned. As well as looking at the stars, I went along with it. When night finally fell, the stars came out. I wrote down every single one, and as I looked at the stars and wrote about them, I could tell she wanted to say something but kept it from me. I started off with the leading question that got her to talk to me. She was very hesitant but asked if we could stay for a lot longer. I looked at her with some shock but didn't know how to answer. Instead, I took a sip of tea, but as I put it down, Colette told me to open the letter, When I was

25 Letters Later

about to open it, her lip suddenly touched mine. I looked for a while, and
tried to talk but before I could say anything she ran off.

CHAPTER 9

As I saw Colette run, I called her name, but she never turned back. I sat back down, not knowing and processing what just happened. I grab the letter she left for me. I put it off a little before opening it, wondering if I really should. As I opened it the letter read.

"Dear Best friend

Every day I thought about you, I didn't know what I felt for you, but every time I saw you my heart was happy and I smiled big. If I knew you didn't feel the same way, I wouldn't have kissed you two times that night. Either way, if you wanted to be with me, I ran to the lake we passed not too long ago. I'll wait for u there if you decide to come, but I understand if you don't want to. If you look in the basket, there is a present for you. It's something that I made that you enjoy. If you like me the way, I like you to come to see me.

Your Colette."

I thought hard, but I opened the basket, to my surprise it was the cake I've always loved from Colette. I got up and started to run to the lake, I knew I kept stuff from Colette, but I did like her more than she knew. I loved her company when she would come over. I never got tired of her dancing and her getting close to me. Now I feel like I blew it with her. I ran as fast as I could till I saw her sitting alone by the lake. I called out her name. To my surprise, Colette turned around with a smile. As I ran to her, she put her arms out, and I jumped into her and put my lips on hers. All the birds chirped, and the bugs buzzed as she held me in her arms tightly. After a few minutes, I took her hands and apologized for being so blunt and not knowing she felt the same way I did. As Colette and I returned to the picnic, our puppy came running to us. Colette took my chin and pulled me in for another kiss. This time, it felt like we were a family with her puppy. I smiled as we laid back down. I told Colette that my mother always knew something. She laughed, put her arms around me, and soon fell asleep as the stars came out. Before I fell asleep, I wondered what my mother would think about us together, but not long after, I was asleep dreaming of a home with me and Colette. I dreamt about how we would spend the rest of our days together. We both knew we would rather go home again and be together forever till we died, but we also knew it was not accepted yet. I work up for a little. And gave Colette a kiss on the forehead and put

Ally Molison

her arms around me to feel safe and happy. I closed my eyes one last time before everything was dark again.

CPSIA information can be obtained
at www.ICGtesting.com
Printed in the USA
BVHW041206111022
649148BV00015B/995/J